BACK HOME

by **GLORIA JEAN PINKNEY**

• pictures by **JERRY PINKNEY** •

Dial

Books

for

Young

Readers

New York

Published by Dial Books for Young Readers
A Division of Penguin Books USA Inc.
375 Hudson Street
New York, New York 10014
Text copyright © 1992 by Gloria Jean Pinkney
Pictures copyright © 1992 by Jerry Pinkney
Printed in the U.S.A.
First Edition
3 5 7 9 10 8 6 4 2

Library of Congress Cataloging in Publication Data
Pinkney, Gloria Jean.
Back home / by Gloria Jean Pinkney; pictures by Jerry Pinkney.
p. cm.
Summary: Eight-year-old Ernestine returns
to visit relatives on the North Carolina
farm where she was born.
ISBN 0-8037-1168-9.—ISBN 0-8037-1169-7 (lib. bdg.)
[1. Farm life—Fiction. 2. North Carolina—Fiction.]
I. Pinkney, Jerry, ill. II. Title.
PZ7.P6334Bac 1992 [E]—dc20 91-22610 CIP AC

*The full-color artwork was prepared using pencil,
colored pencils, and watercolor.
It was then color-separated and reproduced as
red, blue, yellow, and black halftones.*

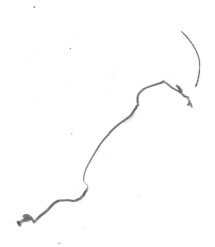

To Jerry, Uncle Thomas, and in memory
of my mother, Ernestine
G. J. P.

•

To Gloria Jean with great affection
and admiration
J. P.

Ernestine recognized Uncle June Avery right away. She remembered Mama saying, "He'll probably bring you flowers." He also had the same sparkling eyes and apple-dumpling cheeks as Grandmama Zulah in Mama's old photograph.

He was waiting on the platform as the Silver Star slowly pulled into Robeson County Depot. When he caught a glimpse of Ernestine peering through the window, his face lit up in a broad smile.

Ernestine smiled back. "Uncle June!" she cried, waving to her great-uncle. Then she straightened her new organdy pinafore, grabbed her satchel, and hurried to the exit.

Her legs felt wobbly from the long train ride south. But that didn't bother Ernestine Avery Powell. She was in Lumberton, North Carolina—the place where she was born—for the first time in her memory.

"Hey, Ernestine!" said Uncle June, lifting her satchel. "I knew right off it was you. I do declare," he exclaimed, "if you don't favor my oldest sister Zulah when she was a girl."

Ernestine felt warm inside. I look like Grandmama! she thought.

"I picked these here flowers for you," he said, "fresh this morning from my garden."

"Thank you, Uncle June. It was real nice of you and Aunt Beula to invite me."

"Well," he said, "we think it only fitting that you get to know your kinfolk. Was the train ride to your liking?"

"Oh, yes!" Ernestine cried.

"Come on," said Uncle June. "My truck is right out front. Wait till your Aunt Beula and Cousin Jack see you!"

"Why didn't Jack come with you?" asked Ernestine.

"Well," said Uncle June, "Jack had his mind set on riding with me today, but his new kid was born this morning."

"I know all about Jack and his goats. Aunt Beula told us in her letters." I hope Jack will like me, she thought.

Uncle June walked up to an old truck.

"Ole Lizzie!" Ernestine shouted, jumping up and down and dancing all around it. "Mama used to ride to the schoolhouse in the back of this pickup truck, didn't she, Uncle June?"

"Every day," he replied.

Ernestine's eyes lit up. "May I ride in back too?" she asked.

Uncle June laughed. "I think you'd best wait, and change out of them fancy clothes first."

She climbed right onto the front seat. "Is it a long ride to the farm, Uncle June?"

"We're just a few miles down Sandy Bottom," he said, pulling onto the road.

While they rode along, Ernestine studied the green country-side. "It's so quiet here," she said. "Not anything like the city."

"I never did take to city life myself," Uncle June responded. "After your folks moved up North, we paid you all a visit. You and Jack were still babies then." He pulled into a long driveway and turned the engine off.

Ernestine looked at the old wooden farmhouse, then jumped down onto the soft ground, pulled off her shoes, and wiggled her toes in the warm North Carolina sand. "I'm here!" she shouted happily.

When Aunt Beula saw Ernestine, dressed in her fancy frock, carrying her flowers in one hand and shoes in the other, she laughed until the tears flowed. "How I wish your Grandmama Zulah could see you today, Ernestine!" said Aunt Beula. "Zulah never did take to wearing no shoes! Come here, chile," she said, "and give your Aunt Beula some sugar!"

Suddenly Jack came running from the shed. "Hey, Cousin Ernestine!" he said, crinkling up his face. "I was gonna show you my new kid, but not in them fancy clothes."

Ernestine felt disappointed. "Mama made me lots of play clothes, Jack," she said.

"Ernestine can see that goat tomorrow," Aunt Beula called out. "You all come on in now. Supper's on!"

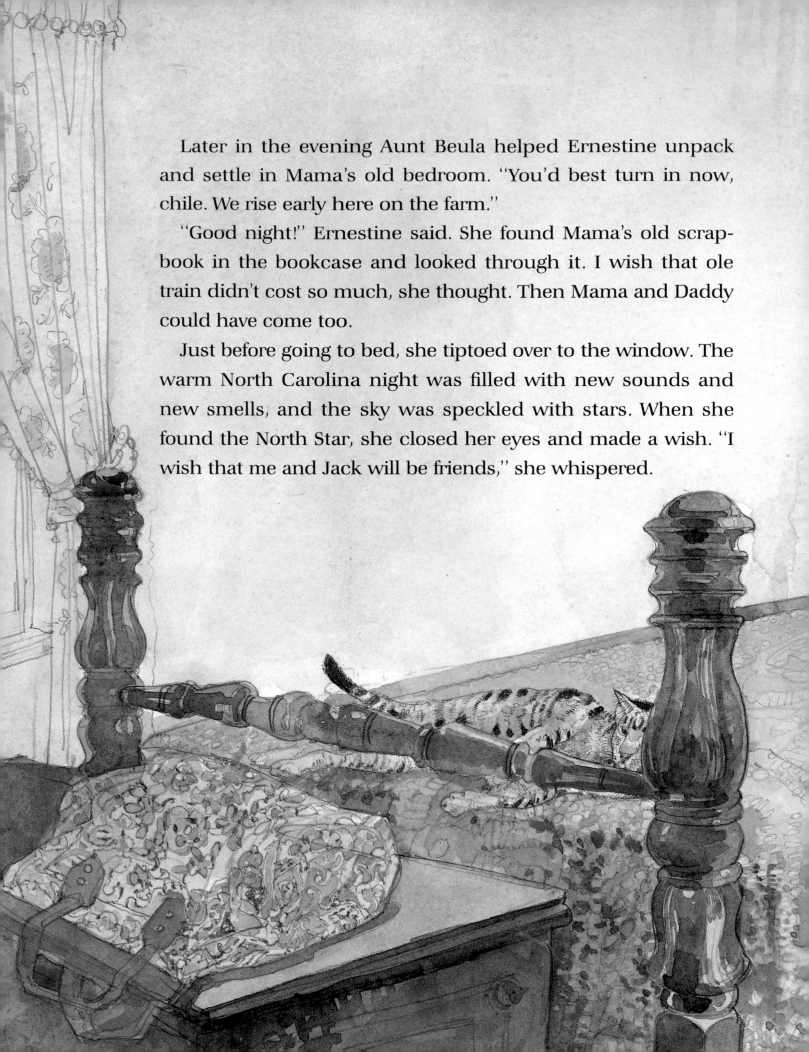

Later in the evening Aunt Beula helped Ernestine unpack and settle in Mama's old bedroom. "You'd best turn in now, chile. We rise early here on the farm."

"Good night!" Ernestine said. She found Mama's old scrapbook in the bookcase and looked through it. I wish that ole train didn't cost so much, she thought. Then Mama and Daddy could have come too.

Just before going to bed, she tiptoed over to the window. The warm North Carolina night was filled with new sounds and new smells, and the sky was speckled with stars. When she found the North Star, she closed her eyes and made a wish. "I wish that me and Jack will be friends," she whispered.

It was dawn. Soft voices and the sweet scent of freshly baked biscuits drifted up from the kitchen. Ernestine heard someone humming. She ran to the window and looked out. Uncle June was hitching his mule to the plow. "Good morning, Uncle June!" she called out.

He looked up and smiled. "Morning, Ernestine! You're up right early for a city girl."

Ernestine giggled. She dressed in her new pedal pushers and hurried down to the kitchen. After breakfast she helped her aunt with the kitchen chores, then headed straight for the door.

"It's awful dusty in the shed, chile," Aunt Beula called. "I think you'd best change into your overalls first."

"I don't have any overalls, Aunt Beula," she said. "Mama won't let me wear them at home."

"Well," said her aunt, "let's see what we can find in your grandmama's ole steamer trunk." They went upstairs. Aunt Beula pulled out a pair of overalls from the trunk. "These used to be your mama's when she was a girl," she said. "They're a bit worn, but they'll do while you're here."

Ernestine admired herself in the mirror. "Thank you, Aunt Beula," she said and gave her aunt a hug. "I think I'll go see Jack and his baby goat now." She ran downstairs and out to the shed, where she knocked on the door.

"Who is it?" Jack called.

"It's me. Ernestine. May I see your new goat now?" she asked, pulling on the handle. The door didn't budge. It was locked. "Jack Avery," she shouted, "you open up right now!"

"You'll get your fancy clothes dirty!" he teased.

"I have overalls on now," she said. "Open the door and see for yourself."

Slowly Jack opened the door. "You sure look a heap better. Well, I suppose it will be all right." The two older goats followed Jack out into the yard, and he tied them to the fence. "This is Jonah and Rebecca," he said with his chest poked out.

Ernestine followed Jack into the shed. The baby goat was just waking up. "May I hold him?" she asked, gently stroking its head.

"It's not a him, it's a her!" Jack said, laughing at his cousin. "City girls don't know nothing about goats."

Ernestine felt hurt.

Jack gently picked up the baby goat and carried her outside.

Ernestine followed him. "What's her name?" she asked.

Jack pulled two biscuits out of his pocket and began feeding them to Jonah and Rebecca. "I haven't made up my mind yet," he answered.

"How about Princess?" Ernestine suggested.

Jack frowned at his cousin. "Princess!" he said. "That's a citified name!"

"No, it isn't!" Ernestine felt tears spring to her eyes. Embarrassed, she ran back into the house. The rest of the afternoon Jack helped his father weed the flower garden, while Ernestine helped her aunt can peaches in the kitchen.

The next morning at breakfast the children were very quiet. "Don't worry about your chores today, Son," Uncle June said to Jack. "Show your cousin around the farm."

"Yes, Papa!" said Jack. "Come on, Cousin Ernestine," he called. Ernestine followed reluctantly behind him.

Jack went into the feed barn. It was filled with hard corn. He swiftly climbed up the ladder and to Ernestine's surprise, leaped high into the air, his long legs flying onto the grain. Down he rolled, landing smoothly at his cousin's feet.

"Watch me!" said Ernestine, climbing gracefully up the ladder. Taking a deep breath, she sprang, toes pointed, down into the corn. But she didn't roll down. She was stuck fast.

Jack doubled over with laughter. "I knew you couldn't do it," he said, then climbed up and helped her down.

Ernestine didn't reply. She followed him out of the feed barn. Just you wait, Jack Avery, she thought. I'll show you.

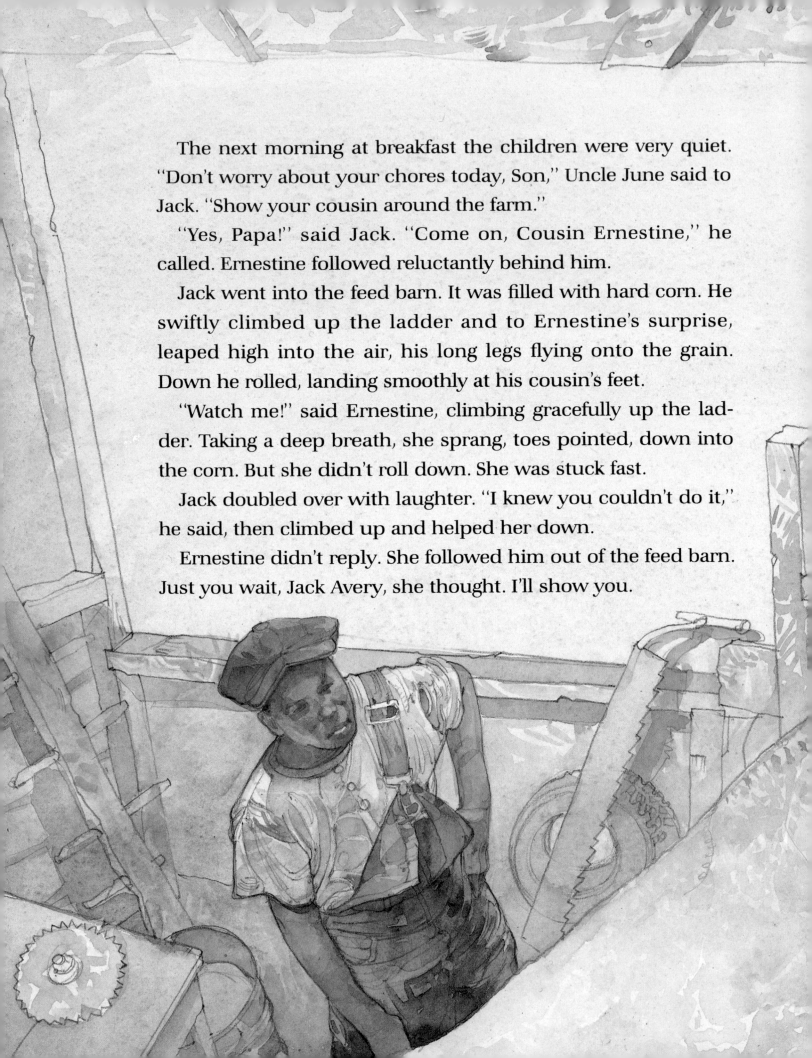

That afternoon Ernestine was sitting on the rail fence watching Jack groom his goats. "I bet you can't ride Jonah," said Jack.

"I can too," Ernestine said.

"Are you sure you're not too scared?"

"I'm not one bit scared, Jack Avery!"

"Well," Jack said, holding Jonah steady for her, "jump on quick and hold on tight."

Ernestine slipped easily onto Jonah's back, and Jack led them around the yard with his rope, grinning from ear to ear.

"Jack Avery!" Aunt Beula called from the house. "You get that chile off that goat right now, before she gets hurt!"

Just then Ernestine lost her grip and fell to the ground, landing with a thud. "Are you all right?" asked Jack.

Ernestine jumped up, brushed herself off, and ran toward the house. Why did I have to fall off? she thought.

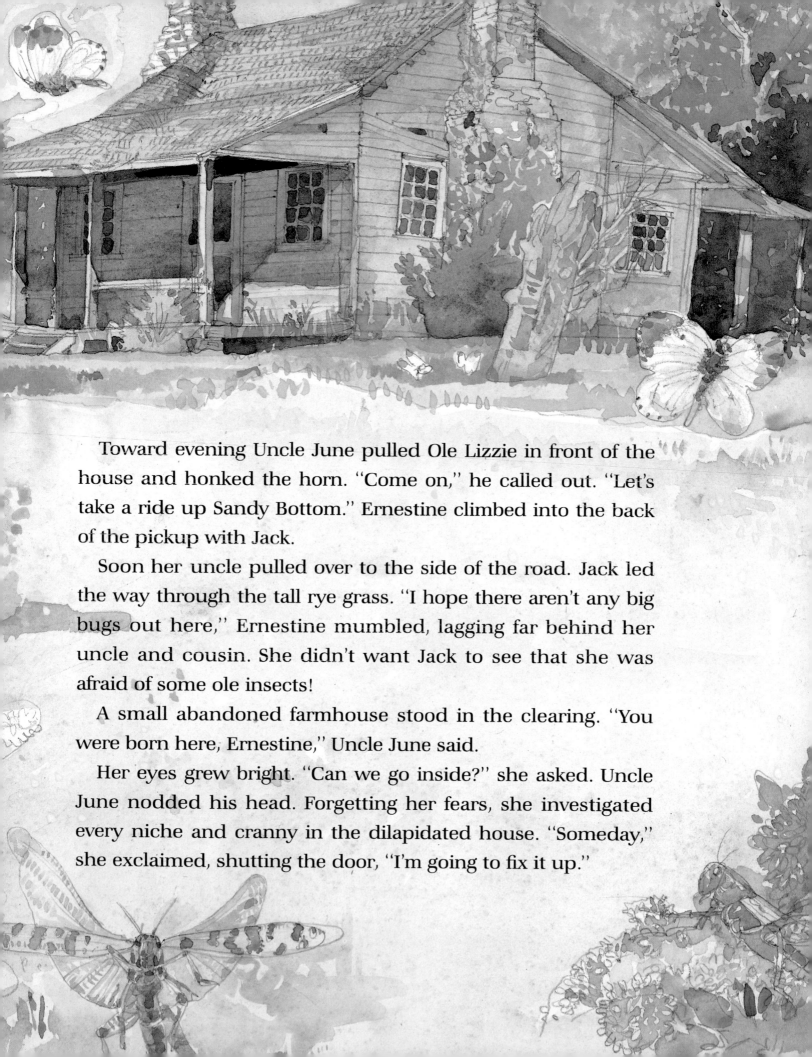

Toward evening Uncle June pulled Ole Lizzie in front of the house and honked the horn. "Come on," he called out. "Let's take a ride up Sandy Bottom." Ernestine climbed into the back of the pickup with Jack.

Soon her uncle pulled over to the side of the road. Jack led the way through the tall rye grass. "I hope there aren't any big bugs out here," Ernestine mumbled, lagging far behind her uncle and cousin. She didn't want Jack to see that she was afraid of some ole insects!

A small abandoned farmhouse stood in the clearing. "You were born here, Ernestine," Uncle June said.

Her eyes grew bright. "Can we go inside?" she asked. Uncle June nodded his head. Forgetting her fears, she investigated every niche and cranny in the dilapidated house. "Someday," she exclaimed, shutting the door, "I'm going to fix it up."

When they arrived back at the farm, she ran straight to the kitchen, flopped herself on the floor, and began to inspect her legs. Aunt Beula watched her for a while. "What you searching for, chile?" she asked.

"Bug bites!" Ernestine replied.

Aunt Beula started laughing. "Ernestine, chile," she said, "you do tickle me so. Don't you know them's Avery bugs out at your old house. They'd never bite their own. Why, they recognized you!"

Ernestine stopped her searching and looked up at her aunt's smiling face. "You're kidding me, Aunt Beula," she said, feeling happy inside.

The first thing she heard the next morning was the sound of church bells. She dressed quickly and hurried downstairs. "Morning, chile," said her aunt. "Did the bells wake you?"

"Yes," said Ernestine.

"Eat your breakfast now, children," said Aunt Beula. "We don't want to be late for church."

They were soon ready to leave. Uncle June gave Aunt Beula a small bouquet and helped her into the pickup. The children climbed into the back. Jack sat in one corner and Ernestine in the other. She was feeling sad. I miss Mama and Daddy, she thought, but I'm not ready to go home today.

Jack leaned over and pulled her hair. "I thought you'd plumb given up on wearing dresses, Cousin Ernestine," he teased.

She frowned at her cousin. "You're a mean boy, Jack Avery," she said. Jack looked sorry but didn't reply.

After the service Aunt Beula gave the flowers to Ernestine. "We thought you might like to visit your grandmama's burial place before you go home," said her aunt.

"I'd like to," Ernestine said softly, "if you hold my hand."

"I will," Jack said, shyly taking her hand. Together the family walked to the Avery Burial Place behind the church. Ernestine read the engraving on Grandmama's marker to herself,

ZULAH THOMPSON
1887–1928

and gently placed the bouquet close to the stone.

Ernestine was quiet on the ride back to the farm. "I wish I could stay a little longer. If only school didn't start next week," she said softly.

Jack grinned at her and said, "I thought up a good name for my goat."

"What is it?"

"I'm going to name her Princess!" he announced.

Ernestine laughed. "You didn't think up that name, Jack Avery. I did!"

After supper Jack went upstairs to help Ernestine with her satchel. "I have a present for you," he said, and gave her a small rawhide pouch.

She loosened the drawstring and looked inside. "Oh," said Ernestine, "the hard corn!"

Jack had a big smile on his face. "So you won't be forgetting the fun we had," he said.

"Thank you, Jack Avery," Ernestine said. She unfastened her satchel and placed the pouch on top. Right on top of Mama's old overalls. Aunt Beula had patched, ironed, and packed the overalls for her to take back to the city. "I'll need these when I come back next summer," she announced. She took them out of the satchel and put them in a drawer.

Just then Uncle June tooted Ole Lizzie's horn. "Time to go, Ernestine," he called. "You wouldn't want to miss your train!"

"Coming, Uncle June!" she called.

Jack picked up her satchel and started downstairs. Ernestine put the scrapbook back on the shelf. Then she took one last look at Mama's room and pulled the door to.

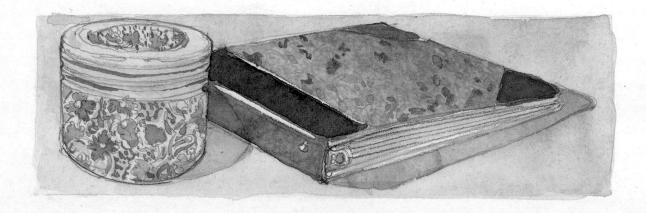